Kyle Goes Alone

By Jan Thornhill

Illustrated by Ashley Barron

Owlkids Books

"I have to go," said Kyle.

Kyle was a three-toed sloth. He lived with his mom high in the rainforest canopy.

Like all sloths, Kyle was a slowpoke.

He moved through the treetops slowly.

He chewed leaves slowly.

He scratched his belly slowly.

Kyle did everything so slowly that he only had to "go" once a week.

And that once a week was…

...NOW.

"You know what?" said his mom. "I think you're old enough to go alone."

"Alone?" said Kyle.

"Uh-huh. Alone."

Kyle looked down toward the ground and shuddered.

Sloths spend their whole lives high in the trees. Sloths never, EVER go down to the ground.

Except when they have to go.

Kyle felt dizzy. The forest floor was a long, LONG, LONG way away. He wasn't sure he was ready to go alone.

"You can do it," said his mom. "I'll be right here if you need me."

So Kyle took a deep breath and started down. He used his hooked claws to slowly lower himself from branch to vine, from vine to tree, from tree to branch.

After what seemed like a very long time, Kyle looked up. He couldn't see his mom anymore.

Maybe he should turn back…except he really had to go.

"You're doing great!" called his mom.

"But I'm all alone!" cried Kyle.

"No, you're not," someone squawked.

It was one of his neighbors,
a red-spectacled parrot.

Kyle wasn't alone after all. So
he started moving down again.

After what seemed like a very long time, Kyle looked up. He couldn't see the red-spectacled parrot. And he couldn't see his mom.

Maybe he should turn back…except now he really had to go.

"Keep moving!" called his mom. "You're almost halfway there!"

"But I'm all alone!" Kyle cried.

"No, you're not," someone hissed.

It was another neighbor, a green and yellow whipsnake.

Kyle wasn't alone after all. The ground looked closer now, too. So he started moving again.

After what seemed like a very long time, Kyle looked up. He couldn't see the green and yellow whipsnake. He couldn't see the red-spectacled parrot. And he couldn't see his mom.

Maybe he should turn back...except now he REALLY had to go.

"Don't stop now!" called his mom. "You've gone so far!"

"But I'm all alone!" Kyle cried.

"No, you're not," someone croaked.

It was another one of Kyle's neighbors, a tiger-legged monkey tree frog.

Kyle wasn't alone after all. And the ground looked even closer now. So he started moving again.

After what seemed like a very long time, Kyle looked up. He couldn't see the tiger-legged monkey tree frog. He couldn't see the green and yellow whipsnake. He couldn't see the red-spectacled parrot. And he couldn't see his mom.

Maybe he should turn back…except now he really, REALLY had to go.

"You're amazing, Kyle!" called his mom. "You're almost there!"

"But I'm all alone!" Kyle cried.

"No, you're not," someone whispered.

It was yet another neighbor, a leaf-cutting ant.
Kyle wasn't alone after all. And the ground
was now so close he could smell it. So he started
moving again.

And then he was there. He'd made it to the forest floor all by himself!

Kyle looked up. He couldn't see the leaf-cutting ant. He couldn't see the tiger-legged monkey tree frog. He couldn't see the green and yellow whipsnake. He couldn't see the red-spectacled parrot. And he couldn't see his mom.

But Kyle didn't care, because he'd made it to the ground…

and he'd made it JUST IN TIME.

Kyle hugged the vine and wiggled back and forth. He closed his eyes.

"How's it going down there?" called his mom.

Kyle was too busy to answer.

"You did it!" squawked the red-spectacled parrot.

"Simply stupendous!" hissed the green and yellow whipsnake.

"Good work, kid!" croaked the tiger-legged monkey tree frog.

"You're awesome!" whispered the leaf-cutting ant.

"I knew you could do it," said his mom.

Now all Kyle had to do was to climb back up to the canopy again.

But the canopy was a long, LONG, LONG way away.

And Kyle was tired.

"You know what?" asked his mom. "I miss carrying you the way I did when you were a baby."

"Really?" said Kyle.

"Really," said his mom.

Kyle was pretty sure he could climb back up to the canopy all by himself. But just to make his mom happy, he let her carry him all the way home.

The Poop about Three-toed Sloths

Three-toed sloths, like Kyle and his mom, live in the rainforests of Central and South America, where they feed mostly on leaves. High in the canopy, they hug trees with their long arms and legs or use their huge hooked claws to hang upside down from branches and vines. They often sleep upside down—and Kyle was even born upside down!

When Kyle was a tiny baby, he would have clung to his mom all the time, nursing and learning which leaves to eat. After a few months, he would begin to explore his surroundings—though at first he'd always keep one foot touching his mom! Kyle will leave his mom for good when he's about six months old, but he won't be fully grown until he's two or three years old. By then he'll be about the size of a large house cat.

Sloths are extremely slow animals. They move slowly, they grow slowly, and they eat slowly. Even their insides move slowly, so it takes a very long time for Kyle and his mom's leafy food to move through their tummies—so long they only have to pee and poo once a week. This is usually the only time sloths make the long journey down to the forest floor. Sloths are helpless on the ground, so they have to hold on tightly to the base of a tree or a vine while they're busy. When they're done, they slowly climb back up to the safety of the treetops and begin eating again.

Camouflage: Hiding in Plain Sight

Did you sometimes have trouble spotting some of the animals in the story? If you did, it's because they were camouflaged. Camouflage is nature's way of helping animals hide by blending in with their surroundings. Being hard to see is useful for hunting animals that need to sneak up on their prey, and for prey animals to hide from hunters.

The simplest camouflage is when an animal has fur, feathers, or scales that match the color of its surroundings. Kyle's mom's brown fur is covered in green algae. The green color makes her hard to see in her rainforest home. The red-spectacled parrot uses camouflage the same way: its green feathers also match the color of the leaves in the forest canopy. Some animals, such as octopuses and chameleons, can actually change their color when they need to match a different background.

Other animals have patterns that help them to disappear. When a tiger-legged monkey tree frog is on the move, his stripes disguise his frog shape. The stripes of an actual tiger make this big cat hard to see when it's moving through a tangle of branches and tall grasses. Other animals, such as owls and moths, have busy patterns that so closely match the bark of trees, they're almost invisible when at rest.

Then there are animals that are such masters of disguise they look like something else entirely. The whipsnake in the story is so long and slender that it can easily pass as a jungle vine. There are also insects that look amazingly like fallen leaves. A few are so leaflike, they look as if they've been nibbled on by other insects!

To my favorite guy, Fred, and to field biologists, who delight me every day with new information about the living things we share this planet with. *~JT*

To Kevin, for his kindness and understanding. *~AB*

Owlkids Books acknowledges the financial support of the Canada Council for the Arts, the Ontario Arts Council, the Government of Canada through the Canada Book Fund (CBF) and the Government of Ontario through the Ontario Media Development Corporation's Book Initiative for our publishing activities.

Published in Canada by
Owlkids Books Inc.
10 Lower Spadina Avenue
Toronto, ON M5V 2Z2

Published in the United States by
Owlkids Books Inc.
1700 Fourth Street
Berkeley, CA 94710

Library and Archives Canada Cataloguing in Publication

Thornhill, Jan, author
    Kyle goes alone / written by Jan Thornhill ; illustrated by Ashley Barron.

ISBN 978-1-77147-075-9 (bound)

    1. Sloths--Juvenile literature. 2. Camouflage (Biology)--Juvenile literature. I. Barron, Ashley, illustrator II. Title.

QL737.E2T46 2015   j599.3'13   C2014-908061-1

Library of Congress Control Number: 2014958763

The artwork in this book was rendered in paper.
The text is set in Adobe Caslon Pro.
Edited by: Jennifer Stokes
Designed by: Barb Kelly
Photography by: Michael Cullen, TPG Digital Art Services

Manufactured in Shenzhen, China, in March 2015,
by C&C Joint Printing Co.
Job #201500166R1

A   B   C   D   E   F

Publisher of Chirp, chickaDEE and OWL
www.owlkidsbooks.com

Sources

Soares, C.A. and Carneiro, R.S. (2001) "Social behavior between mothers and young of sloths." *Brazilian Journal of Biology*, 62(2): 249–252.

Ramirez, O., et al. (2011) "Temporal and spatial resource use by female three-toed sloths and their young in an agricultural landscape in Costa Rica." *Revista de Biologia Tropical*, 59(4): 1743–1755.

Craig Holdrege. "What Does It Mean to Be a Sloth?" http://natureinstitute.org/nature/sloth.htm.

Brady Bullinger. "Bradypus torquatus—maned three-toed sloth." http://animaldiversity.ummz.umich.edu/accounts/Bradypus_torquatus.

Sloth Sanctuary Costa Rica, http://www.slothsanctuary.com/blog.

"Baby Sloths Get Potty Trained" (video), http://www.animalplanet.com/tv-shows/too-cute/videos/baby-sloths-get-potty-trained.